UNICORN RIDERS

We Ride As One

To my children and all those who believe in unicorns — AD
To my children, Clare and Max — JB

Picture Window Books are published by Capstone,
1710 Roe Crest Drive, North Mankato, Minnesota 56003
www.mycapstone.com

Library of Congress Cataloging-in-Publication Data
Names: Darlison, Aleesah, author. | Brailsford, Jill, illustrator.
Title: Willow's challenge / by Aleesah Darlison ; [Jill Brailsford, illustrator].
Description: North Mankato, Minnesota : Picture Window Books, an imprint of
  Capstone Press, [2017] | Series: Unicorn Riders | Summary: Head Rider
  Willow is sent on a mission to Arlen to bring a healing elixir to Lord
  Gildenfair, her uncle, whom she hates because she believes he ruined her
  family—but the Unicorn Riders arrive to find Arlen is under attack, and
  Willow must confront her past and find a way to save the city.
Identifiers: LCCN 2016008024 | ISBN 9781479565450 (library binding) |
  ISBN 9781479565535 (paperback) | ISBN 9781479584840 (ebook (pdf))
Subjects: LCSH: Unicorns—Juvenile fiction. | Magic—Juvenile fiction. |
  Uncles—Juvenile fiction. | Memory—Juvenile fiction. | Adventure stories.
  | CYAC: Unicorns—Fiction. | Magic—Fiction. | Uncles—Fiction. |
  Memory—Fiction. | Adventure and adventurers—Fiction. | GSAFD:
Adventure fiction.
Classification: LCC PZ7.1.D333 Wi 2017 | DDC 813.6—dc23
LC record available at http://lccn.loc.gov/2016008024

Editor: Nikki Potts
Designer: Bobbie Nuytten
Art Director: Nathan Gassman
Production Specialist: Katy LaVigne
The illustrations in this book were created by Jill Brailsford.

Cover design by Walker Books Australia Pty Ltd
Cover images: Rider, symbol and unicorns © Gillian Brailsford 2011;
lined paper © iStockphoto.com/Imageegaml;
parchment © iStockphoto.com/Peter Zelei

The illustrations for this book were created with black pen,
pencil, and digital media.

Design Element: Shutterstock: Slanapotam

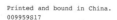

UNICORN RIDERS

Willow's Challenge

Aleesah Darlison

Illustrations by
Jill Brailsford

PICTURE WINDOW BOOKS
a capstone imprint

Willow & Obecky

Willow's symbol
- a violet—represents being watchful and faithful

Uniform color
- green

Unicorn
- Obecky has a black opal horn.
- She has the gifts of healing and strength.

Ellabeth & Fayza

Ellabeth's symbol
- a hummingbird—represents energy, persistence, and loyalty

Uniform color
- red

Unicorn
- Fayza has an orange topaz horn.
- She has the gift of speed and can also light the dark with her golden magic.

Quinn & Ula

Quinn's symbol
- a butterfly—represents change and lightness

Uniform color
- blue

Unicorn
- Ula has a ruby horn.
- She has the gift of speaking with Quinn using mind-messages.
- She can also sense danger.

Krystal & Estrella

Krystal's symbol
- a diamond—represents perfection, wisdom, and beauty

Uniform color
- purple

Unicorn
- Estrella has a pearl horn.
- She has the gift of enchantment.

The
Unicorn Riders' World

The Unicorn Riders of Avamay

Under the guidance of their leader, Jala, the Unicorn Riders and their magical unicorns protect the Kingdom of Avamay from the threats of evil Lord Valerian.

Decades ago, Lord Valerian forcefully took over the neighboring kingdom of Obeera. He began capturing every magical creature across the eight kingdoms. Luckily, King Perry saved four of Avamay's unicorns. He asked the unicorns to help protect Avamay. And that's when ordinary girls were chosen to be the first Unicorn Riders.

A Rider is chosen when her name and likeness appear in The Choosing Book, which is guarded by Jala. It holds the details of all the past, present, and future Riders. No one can see who the future Riders will be until it is time for a new Rider to be chosen. Only then will The Choosing Book display her details.

• CHAPTER 1 •

WITH A CLICK OF her tongue and a nudge of her knees, Willow set her unicorn into a trot. Bending low over Obecky's sleek neck, Willow gave a sharper nudge. Obecky cantered faster.

The wind rushed over Willow's face and through her honey-brown hair. The smells of the late spring afternoon — buttercups, daisies, and crushed grass — rushed to greet her. But Willow didn't have time to enjoy them. Not now.

"Faster, Obecky, faster," she said as she urged the unicorn into a gallop. "I'm Head Rider. I have to set the pace for the others."

Obecky sped up, enjoying the race as much as her Rider. Willow didn't use a bridle or a saddle.

Unicorns couldn't stand the touch of either, and it was against the Riders' Code to use them.

Willow felt the gold token digging into the palm of her hand. She had to make it to the box and slip the token in before time ran out.

They splashed through the bubbling creek, then up and over the last rise toward the finish line. Willow spotted the other Riders. Krystal, Ellabeth, and tiny Quinn were hanging over the fence railings, cheering her on while their unicorns grazed nearby.

The Riders were dressed in their uniforms as usual. Krystal's uniform was purple, her symbol a sparkling diamond. Quinn's uniform was pale blue with the symbol of a butterfly embroidered on the front. Ellabeth was dressed in red, and her symbol was a hummingbird.

Willow glanced down at her green uniform and violet emblem. Her violet stood for watchfulness and faith. Like all Riders' symbols, it had been chosen for her by Jala, the Unicorn Riders' leader, when Willow had arrived at Keydell.

Focusing again on the task at hand, Willow smiled with determination as she neared the obstacle course. Each week, Jala set up this course for the Riders. It was part of their training. Rickety bridges and deep, muddy gullies were part of the course. The obstacles were designed to test both the girls and the unicorns. The course was meant to prepare them for dangers on their missions to protect the kingdom of Avamay. Together, Rider and unicorn had to be quick enough to beat the clock. But they also had to be steady enough to handle the distractions of the course.

Obecky was always calm and confident during training, and they were making good time. Willow was certain they would beat Ellabeth and Fayza.

Fayza was the fastest unicorn in the stable and was always hard to beat.

"Come on, girl," Willow said. "I think we've got 'em."

As Willow reached out to drop the token in the box, Obecky squealed and reared on her hind legs. It took all of Willow's strength to stay on her unicorn.

"Easy, girl!" Willow cried, accidentally dropping the token as she clutched at Obecky's long mane.

Then Willow saw it. A greasly was slithering and hissing in the grass right at Obecky's feet.

Although a greasly looked like a snake, it had three heads. And while a snake might slither away to save its skin, a greasly's first instinct was to bite and keep biting.

This is a bad omen, Willow thought.

• CHAPTER 2 •

THE OTHER RIDERS ALSO saw the greasly and ran shouting in all directions. At the sound of their shouts, Jala came running from the stables.

Is this part of the test? Willow wondered.

"It's all right, girl," Willow said. "Steady now."

Obecky wouldn't listen. She was too frightened. The greasly hissed and snapped and slithered closer to Obecky.

Each unicorn had her own unique magical abilities. Obecky's special skill was to be able to calm and heal others.

"Obecky, use your magic," Willow said firmly to her unicorn.

Somehow, Willow's words got through.

Obecky pranced backward and sent a cloud of gray-blue sparks from her black opal horn directly at the greasly. The magic fell into the its three open mouths. It hissed once more and then went calm.

Obecky's magic had worked.

Willow slid off Obecky's back as Old Elsid, the groundskeeper, came running. He carried a hooked stick and a cloth bag.

"Move back, lass," Old Elsid said. "I'll handle this."

"Oh, it smells terrible," Willow gasped.

Elsid nodded. "Yes," he said. "As if their venom ain't enough defense, that smell keeps predators away, too. Highly unique, wouldn't you say?"

Willow held her nose. "Sure is," she said.

Old Elsid hooked his stick around the greasly's necks and tucked it into the bag. "It won't bother you any more," he said. "I'll take it back to the forest."

Jala and the other Riders ran over, their unicorns stepping cautiously behind them. No one liked greaslies.

"Hideous creature," Quinn said. "What's it doing here? They don't normally come out of the forest."

"It's a bad omen, that's what it is," Krystal said as she stroked Estrella to calm her. "Wherever greaslies go, bad luck follows."

Willow nodded. "That's right," she said.

"What nonsense," Ellabeth snorted. "That's an old wives' tale."

"Don't believe us then," Krystal snapped.

Jala shot Ellabeth and Krystal a warning look. The two girls often argued. "Enough, you two," Jala said as she turned to study Willow. "Are you all right?"

"I'm fine," Willow said. "It's just . . . of all the creatures in the world, greaslies are my least favorite."

Jala's reply was interrupted by a screech from overhead. Everyone looked up.

"It's Belmont," Krystal said, squinting into the sun.

Jala whistled. A gray and white falcon circled above their heads before flapping in to land on Jala's outstretched arm, his long talons curling almost all the way around her wrist.

The falcon was a trained messenger. When he wasn't soaring high, searching for prey, he was usually delivering messages to townships throughout the kingdom of Avamay.

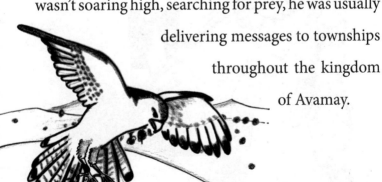

The girls crowded around their leader.

"Has he got a message?" Ellabeth asked. "What does it say?"

"Hold your unicorns," Krystal said.

While the two girls argued, Jala untied a leather strap from Belmont's leg. Wrapped within was a tiny scroll of white paper.

Jala unfurled the note.

Kind Riders, I ask for your help. I have been struck down by a mysterious illness. Not knowing who to trust here, I have sent this secret message to you by your kestrel. Please take pity on me, and send the Neroli Elixir as soon as you can. It is my only hope. Flossy knows the way to Arlen, if she will come.

Yours,
Lord Greyson Gildenfair

Willow suddenly felt cold. Lord Gildenfair. *Krystal and I were right,* she thought. *Greaslies are a bad omen.*

"Arlen? Isn't that where you're from, Willow?" Krystal asked.

"I was," Willow said. "Once."

"Do you know Lord Gildenfair?" Jala asked.

"Yes," Willow replied, unable to meet Jala's eye. "I know him. Arlen is a small place, after all."

"And a lord is an important man to his people," Jala added.

"Lord Gildenfair is more self-important than anything else," Willow muttered.

"What do you mean?" Ellabeth asked.

Willow shrugged. "Just take my word for it," she said.

"He must be ill if he's asking for the Neroli Elixir," Jala said. "It should only ever be used in special situations, when all other possibilities of healing have failed. The ingredients are so strong that the elixir may harm people. Some have even been known to die from taking it. That's why the Unicorn Riders guard the recipe for the elixir. It should only be used under strict control." Jala eyed the girls seriously. "Lord Gildenfair must be desperate."

Krystal frowned. "I wonder why he doesn't trust his own doctors?" she asked.

"Beats me," Willow said.

"The message mentions someone named Flossy. Was your name once Flossy, Willow?" Jala asked.

Willow coughed. "Um, I'd better take Obecky up to the stables," she said. "I want to make sure she's all right after her run-in with that greasly."

Willow turned and strode away, whistling to Obecky as she went. With a swish of her tail, Obecky fell into step beside her Rider. Willow could feel Jala and the other girls' eyes on her as she walked away, but she didn't care. She didn't look back either.

They can think what they want, Willow thought. *I can't go back to Arlen. Not now. Not ever.*

Obecky nudged Willow's shoulder.

Willow hugged her unicorn's neck. "You always understand me, don't you, girl?" she said.

Willow felt the vibration deep in Obecky's throat as she nickered.

"I knew you would," Willow said.

• CHAPTER 3 •

JALA FOUND WILLOW BRUSHING Obecky in the stables. "Are you going to explain what that was all about?" Jala asked.

"I don't know what you mean," Willow replied, keeping her face blank.

Jala shot Willow a severe look. "I expect more from you as Head Rider, Willow," she said.

"Like what?" asked Willow.

"Like honesty. Who is Lord Gildenfair?" asked Jala.

Willow sighed. "He is the most powerful man in Arlen," she said. "He owns the city. The people. Everything." Willow glanced up at Jala, her cheeks flaming and her eyes dark with anger. "He's my uncle. My mother's brother. He's not a nice man." She twisted her hands together, trying not to cry.

"But he's asking for our help. Or Flossy's help, to be more precise," Jala said as she studied Willow carefully. "I'll ask you again, are you Flossy?"

"I don't want to help him," Willow said. "I don't have to, do I? He wouldn't help my father though he begged him to. He ruined our family." Her voice strangled in her throat. Her chin trembled as a tear trickled down her cheek. "He's a cruel, horrible man. He doesn't deserve my help," Willow said brushing away the tear.

"So you *are* Flossy?" Jala asked again.

Willow shrugged. "It's a nickname he had for me. I don't know why he would still use it," she said.

"The man appears to be on his deathbed, Willow. He wants to see you," Jala said.

"He just wants to save his skin," replied Willow.

"This is a special mission for you, Willow," Jala said. "A personal mission. I think you need to face your uncle and your past."

"I can't," Willow said as she swiped at her eyes. She was afraid of going back to Arlen. Afraid of facing her uncle. "I'm needed here."

"It will do you good to see your home again," said Jala. "Besides, your uncle needs your help."

"I will never help him! Never!" shouted Willow.

Willow glanced up to see the other Riders creeping into the stables.

"I'm sorry," Krystal said blushing. "We overheard what you were saying."

Willow covered her mouth in shame. "You must think I'm awful," Willow said.

"It's okay," Quinn said as she put her arm around Willow's shoulders. "We're on your side."

"Maybe your uncle wants to explain," Krystal said. "Maybe he wants your forgiveness."

"He'll be waiting a long time," Willow said, pulling herself together. "Forgiveness is for the weak, and I am not weak. I am a Unicorn Rider."

"You're wrong," Ellabeth said. "I mean, Unicorn Riders are strong, it's true, but you're not weak if you forgive."

"Who says?" Willow asked.

"Family is important," Quinn said softly. "The most important thing of all. You should go."

Willow knew Quinn was sensitive about family. Quinn had been left at an orphanage as a baby and had never known her mother or father growing up. Even when she had met her father and sister, they hadn't wanted to know her. Her family's rejection had affected Quinn deeply.

In her heart, Willow knew Quinn was right, but she didn't want to agree with her. Her anger made her feel strong. If she stayed angry, she wouldn't have to face her uncle or relive the terrible things that had happened. She wouldn't have to face being hurt again.

The dinner bell sounded, interrupting them. Jala and the Riders wandered up to the dining hall while Willow stalked unhappily behind. After washing their faces and hands, they took their places around the large oak table in the dining room. Alda, the cook, bustled about making sure the girls had enough to eat and drink.

"Why don't we all go to Arlen?" Ellabeth said.

"I'm not going," Willow said.

"Your uncle needs you," said Quinn. Her blue eyes pleaded with Willow. "You know you have to go. Besides, the note was addressed to all of us. We're all responsible."

"That's right. We should all go," Ellabeth agreed. "We're Unicorn Riders, and we ride as one."

"I agree with Ellabeth," Krystal said.

I don't want to go, Willow thought.

Willow pushed her food around her plate. Memories of her uncle turned the food in her stomach. She looked at the other Riders, their eyes bright, urging her to change her mind.

What can I do? I'm Head Rider. I must do the right thing, Willow thought.

"I really don't want to go," Willow said slowly, "but deep down something tells me it's the right thing to do." She smiled sadly at the others. "This journey will be hard for me, which is why I'd love it if all of you would come along, too. I have a feeling I'm going to need your support."

"Yay!" Ellabeth cheered. "We ride as one!"

• CHAPTER 4 •

AFTER A RESTLESS NIGHT'S sleep, Willow rose at dawn to prepare Obecky for the journey. She put the elixir, which Jala had given her the night before, in her uniform pocket. She could feel its weight against her hip.

Jala and the other girls met Willow in the courtyard where the Unicorn Riders always gathered before a mission. Willow slung her backpack over her shoulder, and Jala pressed a small, round object into her hand.

Willow looked down and saw a purple amethyst tied onto a leather strap. But this wasn't an ordinary amethyst. It had been carefully engraved with an image of a violet, Willow's symbol.

"It's an amulet," Jala said.

"It's so beautiful," Willow said as she traced the delicate pattern of the violet with her finger. "How did you make it? It must be very precious."

"But most precious to you," Jala said. She helped Willow tie the amulet around her neck. "Your violet symbol will watch over you and protect you as you travel."

Willow felt a warmth coming from the amulet as it rested in the hollow of her throat. "Is it magic?" she asked.

Jala kept many magical things. The secrets were passed from leader to leader and the magic often came in handy for the Riders.

"Yes," Jala replied. "If you're ever in doubt, or in need, wish on the amulet, and it will help you find a way through your troubles."

Jala was always so good and kind to her. Willow took a deep breath and blinked her tears away, refusing to give in to them. "Thank you," Willow said.

"One more thing," Jala said as she rested her hand on Willow's shoulder. "This journey won't be easy for you, but please remember that only the strong can find it in their hearts to forgive. And you, my friend, are one of the strongest people I know — in here." She pointed to Willow's heart.

Willow gulped but didn't say anything. She didn't know if she believed what Jala had just said.

If I'm so strong, why am I so afraid? she wondered.

Willow knew Jala expected a lot from her as Head Rider. She knew the other girls looked up to her. Sometimes she wished she didn't always have to be so responsible or dependable, but now wasn't the time to say anything.

She was dreading the mission, but she was glad the other Riders were going with her. It was comforting to know that she could always depend on them.

"Do we ride as one?" Willow asked, sounding more cheerful than she felt.

"We ride as one," the Riders replied together.

They trotted out of the estate and through the empty early morning streets of Keydell, heading south to Arlen. The unicorns' hooves echoed across the cobblestones. Willow knew she had made the right decision in letting the other Riders go with her. She would have been lonely without them.

Up hillsides and across great, grassy plains, the unicorns galloped. By late afternoon, Willow began

to recognize the familiar landmarks leading to her old home.

"We're getting close," Willow told the others.

Before reaching Arlen, the Riders came upon a forest called Tivia Wood. There the path grew soft, the trees thickened, and the air cooled. Willow and the other Riders trotted beneath the shadowy canopy. Childhood memories flooded back to Willow. She had spent many hours wandering these woods with her best friend, Calder Brock. Willow would often go

into the woods with Calder to take his father, a woodcutter, his lunch.

Willow smiled. She'd missed Calder terribly since leaving Arlen. It had been so long since she'd seen him. She wondered whether he had changed. Seeing Calder again was the only part of returning home Willow was looking forward to. *What had become of him? Would he remember her?*

Reluctantly, Willow thought of her uncle, too. He hadn't tried to contact her after she had left Arlen, not even when she had become a Rider. When that happened, it had been announced throughout the kingdom.

Suddenly, Quinn signaled for everyone to stop. She glanced around carefully. "Ula has picked up on something," she whispered. "She says danger is heading this way."

Ula had a special skill for sensing danger. She communicated with Quinn through mind-messages. More than once, Ula's gift had saved the Riders.

"Okay," Willow said. "Up there, quick!" She motioned for the others to follow her off the path. The Riders dismounted and then hid with their unicorns behind a boulder and thick ferns.

The sound of approaching horses and the jangle of harnesses sliced through the silence of the forest.

Behind the boulder, the Riders watched as a group of men filed past. There were several hundred of them, all heavily armed with spears and bows and arrows. Five pairs of horses pulled heavy carts loaded with more weapons and supplies.

"Soldiers," Ellabeth hissed.

Willow didn't recognize the coat of arms on the men's armor. It showed a black panther pouncing. On top of the panther was a shining silver sword.

"Do you think they belong to Lord Valerian?" Krystal whispered.

Lord Valerian was the evil ruler of the neighboring kingdom of Obeera. He was always causing problems for the Riders and threatening to invade Avamay. No one knew where or when he might strike.

Willow placed a finger to her lips. The girls went back to watching the soldiers as they filed past, leaving two men to bring up the rear. One of them was dressed in clothes far more colorful and well-made than the others. It was clear he was the leader and a wealthy man. His helmet was made of gold, as was his horse's harness.

"We must be getting close," the man in the gold helmet said. He was young, only in his early twenties, and handsome. He had wavy, golden hair and a neatly trimmed golden beard. His blue eyes were clear, alert, and very, very hard.

"Do you think they suspect anything, Lord Elsen?" the other asked.

"Not a thing," Lord Elsen replied. "We'll set up camp a little farther from here, and we will let the men rest. We'll attack Arlen at midnight."

Willow's heart caught in her chest. She thought of all the innocent people of Arlen, many of whom she knew and remembered from when she had lived there.

How can we protect them? she thought.

• CHAPTER 5 •

"WHAT WILL WE DO?" Quinn whispered.

"We need to warn the people of Arlen," Ellabeth said adamantly.

"We need to get help," Krystal said.

"We are the help," Ellabeth argued.

"But they're a whole army," Quinn said, chewing her lip. "This is going to be dangerous."

Willow looked at each of the girls in turn. "Quinn is right," Willow said. "It is going to be dangerous, and I'm glad we're all here together. But we don't have time to send for help. We need to warn the townsfolk right away and help them prepare for the attack. This mission just got a whole lot more serious."

But the Riders couldn't go anywhere. The soldiers were camped only a short distance down the road. A lookout was hidden in the bushes nearby. The girls had heard him sneeze and caught a flash of his horse's harness glinting in the sunlight. They couldn't just go riding past the soldiers into Arlen. They would be captured for sure.

Willow racked her brain for a plan. *Surely, there must be some way for us to get past the soldiers?*

Then she remembered another way into Arlen. Few people knew about this route, but she and Calder had often used it as children.

Willow peeked out between the branches of their hiding place. She motioned to the other Riders to remain still and keep the unicorns quiet. She picked up a rock and crept toward the road. Hidden by the ferns, Willow tossed the rock into the bushes behind the man who was the lookout. There was a flash of movement, and then there was rustling as the soldier searched for the source of the noise.

While the lookout was distracted, the Riders leaped onto their unicorns. They trotted down the slope and back the way they had come. They would have gotten away, if it hadn't been for the turkey they startled. It honked loudly.

The lookout heard the honk and turned. Then he spotted them. "Stop!" he cried. "Stop right there."

"Go, girl. Quickly," Willow said urging Obecky on.

She glanced over her shoulder. She saw the soldier leap onto his horse and gallop after her and the other girls. Willow urged Obecky faster.

The other Riders followed Obecky through the forest. Willow leaned low on her unicorn's neck, ducking low-hanging branches and weaving through the trees — just like they did in Jala's obstacle courses.

Her eyes scanned the roadside as she searched for the marker indicating the hidden path.

Where is it? Willow wondered.

Willow's hand slipped to the amulet around her neck. "Please help me find the marker," she said.

The amulet warmed in her hand. It shimmered then sent a ray of golden light piercing through the forest. Ahead in the distance, the light fell on the round, gray rock Calder had put there all those years ago. Willow clearly remembered the day he'd carried it out of the stream. He had huffed and puffed all the way, not letting her help or take a turn carrying it.

Calder had always been like that. Proud and determined.

But Willow couldn't take the secret path through the forest. The soldier was too close and would see them.

Willow's hand found the amulet again. "Hide us now. Please weave your magic," she said.

At once, dark clouds were driven across the sky.

From nowhere, a thick mist appeared. The Riders heard the lookout crashing around on his horse and yelling after them. He was quickly lost in the fog.

"We'll continue on foot," Willow said. "I don't want anyone else getting lost. I think I still remember the way. Stay close."

The Riders slid off their unicorns and walked. Willow and Obecky led the way, carefully picking out the path through the trees. An owl screeched close by, causing Willow to jump. Obecky nickered warily.

"Hey, watch where you're going." Willow heard Krystal mutter through the fog. "You nearly knocked me over," Krystal said.

"Well, if you weren't so slow," Ellabeth grumbled back at her, "I wouldn't be stepping on top of you."

"Quiet, Riders," Willow whispered. "We're not clear of danger yet. You'll give us away."

"It's Ellabeth's fault," Krystal said.

"No it's not," Ellabeth retorted.

"Shhh!" Willow hissed.

The girls fell into an uneasy silence. They continued walking for what seemed like ages.

The words, when they came, were close and loud. "Halt! Who goes there?" asked the unknown voice.

Willow's heart pounded in her chest. She still couldn't see clearly in the fog. Afraid the soldiers had found them, she inched away from the voice.

"I said, halt!" the voice said again.

Willow felt hands grab her. She tried to cry out to the others, tried to tell them to run. Instead, a flash of light burst inside her brain, sending everything black.

• CHAPTER 6 •

WILLOW FELT HERSELF BEING shaken. "Hey, wake up," someone said.

Willow's eyelids felt as heavy as stones. She forced them open and gazed around her.

She was lying on a narrow bed in a simple stone room. The only light came from the fire that burned in the fireplace nearby. A ginger cat sat at the end of the bed mewing at her.

Willow turned toward the voice. A boy, not much older than Willow and dressed in servants' clothes, stared down at her. Krystal stood behind him, watching Willow with a worried look.

"Where am I?" Willow asked. "Where are Obecky and the other Riders?"

"They're outside," Krystal explained. "We thought it best that you lie down for a while. You took a nasty hit."

The boy bowed low. "Honorable Rider," he said, "I apologize for injuring you. You're in the servants' quarters of Lord Gildenfair's castle."

Willow squinted at the boy. "Calder? Is it you?" she asked.

The boy smiled. "Yes, it's me," he said.

"Calder!" Willow said as she jumped up to hug him. "It's me, Willow. You've changed so much. I can't believe it. You're a servant here now?"

Calder blushed, as he slipped out of Willow's embrace. He smoothed down his shirt. "You've changed, too, Honorable Rider," Calder said. "And yes, I'm a servant here now."

"Please, Calder, call me Willow," she said. Willow held a hand to her head where it throbbed. "Oh, my head hurts. What did you do to me?"

Calder looked crushed. "It was an accident, I swear," he said. "I didn't know it was you."

"Yes, of course," Willow said. "I didn't mean to blame you. Oh, Krystal, this is my old friend, Calder. Calder, this is Krystal."

He beamed a huge smile at Krystal as he bowed low. "Honorable Rider," Calder said.

Krystal smiled and took his hand. "Never mind the formalities," she said. "Any friend of Willow's is a friend of mine."

"I need to see Obecky," Willow said, "and I need to see my unc— I mean, Lord Gildenfair."

"Why do you want to see him?" Calder asked. "He destroyed your family, remember?"

"I remember very well," Willow said. "But Lord Gildenfair sent for me. Or rather, he sent for the Neroli Elixir."

"Lord Gildenfair did what?" asked Calder.

"He sent a message for me via Belmont, the Unicorn Riders' falcon," Willow explained. "He said he was ill and needed the Neroli Elixir to cure him."

Calder paced the room. "I suppose a wealthy lord can demand anything of the Riders and get it," he said. "Even while he treats his people so poorly."

"Doesn't he treat you well?" Willow asked.

"See for yourself," Calder replied. "I practically live in a dungeon while he sleeps in a golden bed and drinks from a golden cup. Lord Gildenfair keeps all for himself, but gives nothing to his people."

"After all this time, I hoped he had changed," Willow said.

Calder's laugh held a bitter edge. "It's not possible for a man like Lord Gildenfair to change," he said.

Before Willow could say anything, Calder opened the door and stepped into the hallway. "Never mind all that," said Calder. "You're not here to listen to my troubles. Come, I'll take you to my lord. But please promise you won't tell him I hit you. I'll get into trouble if you do."

Willow sighed and rubbed the spot where her head still throbbed. "Why did you hit me, by the way?" she asked.

"We've been on high alert," said Calder. "There has been talk that our closest neighbor, Lord Elsen, may be working with Valerian. And you know how

Valerian likes to cause trouble. The rumors are that Valerian is trying to create a split within Avamay. If he can't invade from the north, then he will try to cause trouble among the various territories within our borders."

"Divide and conquer . . .," Willow murmured thoughtfully.

"Exactly," Calder said.

"It would be just like Valerian to do something like that," Krystal added.

Calder nodded. "Elsen has been causing lots of problems lately," he said, "burning crops and terrorizing farmers outside the city walls. It's widely believed he's set up a gang of thieves to rob people as they travel to and from Arlen, to ruin our trade. Worst of all, some believe he is planning to attack the city."

The afternoon's events flooded back to Willow. "Not might be. Is," she said. "We saw his soldiers riding toward Arlen earlier."

Calder looked startled. "Quick then. You'd better follow me," Calder said.

They found the other Riders and their unicorns outside. Obecky was there, too. Willow ran to her to make sure she was all right.

"Are you okay?" Quinn asked. "We were worried."

"I'm fine," Willow said. "Just got a little headache."

She explained everything that had happened, including what Calder had said about Lord Elsen.

"What are we going to do?" Ellabeth asked.

"First, I have to see my uncle," Willow said. "Then we have to come up with a plan to deal with Lord Elsen. I'll be back soon. Just sit tight."

"Do you want me to come with you?" Quinn asked. "For a bit of moral support?"

"Thanks. That would be nice," Willow said.

Willow and Quinn followed Calder upstairs to a set of cream-colored double doors, which Calder rapped his knuckles on. Without waiting for a reply, he ushered the Riders inside.

◉ CHAPTER 7 ◉

LORD GILDENFAIR'S CHAMBER WAS large and full of heavy, finely-crafted furniture. The red velvet curtains were pulled wide, the windows propped open, allowing the warm spring air to waft gently into the room. In a far corner stood a huge gold four-poster bed, encrusted with diamonds, its curtains drawn back to reveal a lifeless figure lying within.

Willow thought she should take her boots off, but Calder didn't give her time.

"Lord Gildenfair, your niece, Willow Arkwright, Honorable Unicorn Rider, is here to see you," he said.

"I told you to call me Willow," Willow said as she checked her boots for mud.

51

"I'm sorry, Honorable Rider, I can't," said Calder.

"Calder, we were friends once remember? Equals," Willow said.

"That was a long time ago," he replied.

"Flossy, you came," Lord Gildenfair said. His voice was barely a whisper. He lifted his head weakly from the pillow and then let it drop back down again. "Forgive me for not getting up. I'm afraid I do not have the energy."

Willow glanced helplessly at Quinn.

Quinn squeezed her hand. "I'll be right here. Go on," said Quinn.

Reluctantly, Willow crept closer to the bed where her uncle lay. His eyes were sunken and his cheeks were pale. His hair was silver at the sides and bald on top. Willow could hear his raspy breath and see the sharp rise and fall of his chest as his lungs gasped for air.

Calder strode over to the windows. He shut them firmly and then stood behind Willow, grave and silent.

"Lord Gildenfair?" Willow said. "Is it really you?"

"It is," Lord Gildenfair gasped. "Are you shocked to see me like this?"

Willow couldn't lie. "Yes," she said.

"Ah, Flossy, you always were the sensitive one," said Lord Gildenfair.

Willow frowned. "It's been years since I've been called that. I'd pref—" Willow started to say.

Lord Gildenfair waved Willow away with a bejeweled hand. "You'll always be Flossy to me, my child," he said.

"I'm not your child!" she snapped, her voice rising. She didn't like her uncle calling her by her nickname, not any more. She had to stop herself from stomping her foot. "I'm a Unicorn Rider."

Lord Gildenfair looked pained.

A delightful jolt of satisfaction shot through Willow. Unable to stop herself, she plowed on. "You ruined my family," she said. "You let my father die in jail, and you made my mother leave Arlen. She had to work day and night as a seamstress just to get by. You took everything from us. I hate you!"

"Willow, please, that is not true," Lord Gildenfair said. "I tried to help your father."

"You're lying," Willow said.

Willow felt Quinn's hand on her shoulder. She looked back at the other girl, embarrassed. But Quinn only smiled kindly back at her.

I'm so glad to have her as a friend, Willow thought.

"I'm telling the truth," Lord Gildenfair murmured. He sounded tired and ill, Willow couldn't deny it. "There is much we need to discuss. Much I need to explain now that you are older," he said.

Willow clenched her jaw. "You don't need to explain anything," she said. "I see who you are, and I don't feel sorry for you. My concern at the moment is for Arlen. As we speak, the city is being surrounded by soldiers. They will attack at midnight."

"Elsen," Lord Gildenfair said as he closed his eyes. "How do you know this?"

"We saw his soldiers on their way to Arlen this afternoon," said Willow. "They're heavily armed."

"We must fight them with all we have," Lord Gildenfair said.

"Of course we will," Willow agreed. "The other Riders and I will do all we can to save the city."

"And the elixir? Did you bring it?" her uncle asked.

"I did," Willow replied.

"You must give it to me. I can be up and helping you," said Lord Gildenfair.

Then he began to cough.

Calder stepped forward. "My lord, you should drink the medicine the doctor left you," he said.

"I don't want it," said Lord Gildenfair. "Goodness knows what they've put in that concoction. All it ever does is make me feel more sick."

"Please, my lord, you must follow the doctor's orders," Calder said as he held a small glass of red liquid to Lord Gildenfair's mouth. The old man took a sip then fell back on his pillow.

"Why is Elsen attacking Arlen?" Willow asked.

Lord Gildenfair looked confused. "His father and I always got along, but it seems young Lord Elsen is a brute who thinks he can make his mark by invading other men's lands and taking what is not rightfully his," he said. "Ever since his father died, he has been threatening us. It seems he has finally decided to take action in the most cruel way."

Calder fidgeted at Gildenfair's elbow.

"Please wait outside, Calder," Lord Gildenfair said.

"I'm sorry, my lord," Calder said looking hurt. "I'm only trying to help."

"I said, leave," replied Lord Gildenfair.

Willow bristled. "You shouldn't talk to Calder like that," she said.

Lord Gildenfair started coughing again. Calder sat him up. The sick man clutched at him for support.

Willow felt the amulet around her neck grow hot.

Her hand flew to it, and she held it up. A golden light shone from the violet crystal, landing on the vial of red medicine beside her uncle's bed. She glanced at Calder. He was busy helping Lord Gildenfair and didn't notice. Willow frowned, wondering what the amulet was trying to tell her.

Calder forced the medicine to the old man's lips and made him drink. Within moments Lord Gildenfair had fallen into a deep sleep.

"I'm sorry you had to see that," Calder said. "He can get quite angry. I'm sure you remember his temper."

"I do," she said. "Perhaps I should give him the elixir now." She reached for her pocket once more.

"No," Calder said gently. "The medicine helps a lot, and I doubt you would be able to wake him. If you ask me, he has brought this sickness on himself by being cruel to others."

A knock sounded at the door. It was Ellabeth.

"Willow, you must come quickly," Ellabeth said. "Elsen's army is surrounding the city."

CHAPTER 8

WILLOW, ELLABETH, AND QUINN ran out of the castle.

"Where's Krystal?" Willow asked Ellabeth.

"I told her we'd meet her at the city gates," Ellabeth replied.

"Right," said Willow. "Let's go."

The high stone walls of Arlen stretched all around them. Willow had never realized it before, but now she could see that Arlen was a fortress.

It made Willow remember there were still parts of Avamay that were dangerous. In most areas Avamayans lived peacefully, but not here. Not where greedy lords roamed, trying to invade other lands and claim them for their own. Not where lords were cruel to their people, as Gildenfair apparently was to his.

Thank goodness for the Unicorn Riders! Willow thought.

On their way toward the city gates, the Riders passed a row of cherry blossom trees, their branches heavy with clumps of delicate pink flowers. Behind the trees stood a red stone house. It was the house of Willow's childhood. Memories of her life there seeped into her mind. Some included her uncle turning away from her as she and her mother left Arlen for good. But she also remembered him smiling and pushing her on the rope swing near the back porch and reading to her by the fire.

Willow had a sudden thought. *Had her uncle been kind to her?*

"Come on," Quinn said to Willow. "We must hurry."

Willow glanced around. Night was closing in. So were Lord Elsen and his soldiers.

At the city gates, they found Krystal along with the unicorns and many of the men from the city. Willow recognized some of the faces.

"We thought it best to lock the gates," Krystal told Willow. "Guards are patrolling the walls, and the women and children are being moved deep within the city where they will be safe."

"Excellent," Willow said.

She glanced around at the men collecting weapons and making preparations to defend Arlen. Boys Calder's age and younger were also brought in to

help. They would need as many hands as they could get if Elsen was to be defeated.

"Can Ula tell you anything about the soldiers?" Willow asked Quinn.

Quinn closed her eyes as she communicated with her unicorn. "Ula says we're heavily outnumbered," said Quinn. "Lord Elsen won't be bargained with. His mind is closed and his heart is cold."

Willow raked her hand through her hair. "Anything else?" she asked.

"Only that there are enemies among us," Quinn replied.

"Where?" Krystal asked. "Who?"

"She can't tell," Quinn said, shaking her head. "They're too well hidden."

"I'm not sure how the enemy could be inside the walls already," Willow said. "Perhaps Ula means something else. Keep a lookout for anyone suspicious though."

Willow gathered the men around her to discuss

the upcoming battle. Some of them were seasoned guards and soldiers used to defending their city. They were calm and steady. Others, especially the young boys, were excited and nervous at the prospect of their first battle.

Willow was surprised the townspeople were so loyal to Lord Gildenfair. She had expected most to flee into the countryside or beg to surrender, but all wanted to stay and fight. When she asked the captain of the Arlen army about it, he said, "Lord Gildenfair is good and kind and wise. He helps us prosper and does not tax us unfairly, unlike Lord Elsen."

"Yes," another man agreed, "we've heard stories of Lord Elsen. Of his cruelty and greed. Arlen shan't fall into his hands. Not tonight. Not ever."

The men cheered.

Willow frowned. What the men said didn't match Calder's comments.

She sought Calder out and found him carrying water up to the gates.

"Calder, can I ask you something?" Willow asked.

"Of course. What is it?" Calder replied.

Willow rubbed her forehead. "I'm a little confused," she said. "I asked some of the people why they're loyal to Lord Gildenfair, and they said he was good and kind. They said he treated them fairly, but that's not what you told me."

Calder shrugged. "They don't see everything that goes on in his castle, but I do," he said. "Lord Gildenfair has them all fooled."

"How is that possible?" Willow asked.

"He pays people to lie for him," said Calder. "Besides, they know you're his niece. They're probably too afraid to tell you the truth."

Willow frowned, not quite believing Calder. The men's loyalty had seemed so real and not at all forced. A thread of doubt wove through Willow's mind, but she didn't want to listen to it.

Could Calder be lying to me? Willow wondered as she gazed at Calder.

Still wondering what it all meant, Willow climbed up to look out over the city's walls. She needed to see what the enemy was doing.

But it was dark now, and great clouds gathered in the sky, covering the moon. Besides a few fires in the distance, Willow couldn't see anything.

Willow grasped her amulet. She ran her thumb over the violet etching.

"Please help me see the enemy," she whispered.

Golden light shone like a beacon from the amulet. Instantly, Willow saw the army gathered below in the darkness. She also saw the battalions scattered throughout the forest, either holding their positions in hidden pockets or creeping toward the city.

Willow gasped in shock. Ula had been right. They were far better armed than the men of Arlen.

And there appeared to be more of them than there had been in the afternoon.

Perhaps Lord Valerian had sent more soldiers to help Elsen's army, she thought.

As Willow clambered down from the wall, an icy wind blew across the land, causing her to shiver. Now, more than ever, she would have to stay strong for the people of Arlen and the other Riders. She knew they were depending on her.

"See anything?" Quinn asked.

The other Riders and several of the men gathered around Willow.

"Hundreds of soldiers," Willow said. She tried to keep her voice steady. "This is going to be a tough battle. Perhaps I should ride out and speak to Lord Elsen."

"He's not the type of man to listen," the captain said. "Besides, I'm not letting you go out there. It's far too dangerous. Don't worry, we'll fight them to our last man. We're not afraid of Elsen or his army."

"We'll be right beside you," Willow said. "We have the unicorns and their magic."

"To the Unicorn Riders!" the men cheered.

"Now, everyone, take your places, and follow the captain's orders," Willow said. "Brace yourselves for a long night. We won't let Arlen fall."

The men marched off under the guidance of the captain.

"What are we going to do?" Quinn asked. "We need to find a way to prevent this battle."

"I agree," Krystal said.

"Any ideas?" Willow asked, looking around the group.

"The captain won't let us go out to speak to Lord Elsen," Ellabeth said. "But perhaps we can find some other way to get outside the gates and help."

Willow saw how tired, yet determined, the Riders looked. She knew they all felt the same way. None of them would be able to sit by and see innocent people hurt or the city destroyed.

"Let's wait for our chance, then," Willow said. "And when the time is right, we'll do as we've always done and ride as one."

"Right," the others agreed. "We ride as one!"

• CHAPTER 9 •

WILLOW STOOD OVER LORD Gildenfair as he lay in bed. The other Riders were downstairs making sure the women and children were safe, while the men prepared for battle. Willow had come to give her uncle the Neroli Elixir before Lord Elsen attacked. Before it was too late. She knew it was the right thing to do. It might be her last chance to save him.

Maybe I've been wrong about him, Willow thought. If I help him recover I'll know for sure, because then we can finally talk about all that has happened.

Willow felt the amulet around her neck grow warm. Again the golden light shone from it and landed on the vial of red liquid beside her uncle's bed. Willow picked up the vial up, trying to think back to when everything had changed. She had been so young. . . .

Seeing her old house had brought back memories of a happier time. Willow remembered her uncle playing with her and being kind to her. She knew they were real memories. And she knew from listening to the people that Lord Gildenfair was a good man. Certainly, he had made mistakes years ago, but it seemed he had done much to mend those mistakes. He had changed.

Willow remembered her mother and father arguing. She remembered slamming doors. Her father not coming home as much. She remembered her mother crying day and night. There were countless visits from her uncle. Often he would comfort her mother, holding her while she wept on his shoulder, her tears staining his dark coat.

She sniffed the medicine. There was something awful, something familiar about it. Something Willow couldn't quite recognize. She dipped her little finger into the medicine and tasted it. Nausea washed over her only to evaporate a moment later. *Where had she smelled that scent before?* She racked her brain, but the answer escaped her.

She slipped the vial into her pocket. "Lord Gildenfair?" Willow said.

Her uncle's eyelids flickered, then slowly opened. "Flossy," he replied.

Willow remembered sitting on her uncle's knee by the fire while her mother sewed nearby. She

remembered her mother glancing anxiously out the window.

"It won't make him come home any sooner," her uncle had said.

"I know," Willow's mother replied. "Where is he, Greyson?"

Lord Gildenfair gently slid Willow off his knee and left her sitting in the armchair. He put his arms around his sister and held her while she wept again.

Willow was pulled back into the present by her uncle's voice.

"What is it?" Lord Gildenfair rasped.

"Lord Elsen is set to attack," Willow said.

"Can we defeat him?" asked Lord Gildenfair.

Willow shook her head.

"All you can do is your best, child," he said.

"Before I go," Willow said, "tell me what happened with my family."

Lord Gildenfair cleared his throat. "Are you ready to listen, child?" Lord Gildenfair asked.

Willow nodded.

"I tried to help your father," her uncle said. "He was arrested for not paying his debts, and I didn't do anything to stop it. I thought it would teach him a lesson, but instead your father grew sick in prison and died. Your mother blamed me, and we fought because of it. I was angry with her, and she moved away."

"I did the wrong thing. I know it now," he went on. "I lost everyone who was dear to me, but I promised myself from that moment on I would try to be a better person. And I have tried, Willow. Can you ever forgive me?"

That's when Willow looked inside herself. *Can I forgive him?*

Jala's words came back to her. "Only the strong can find it in their hearts to forgive."

Willow knew now that if she was strong enough, she could forgive. She could forget about the past and move on.

"Uncle, I need to give you the elixir," Willow said.

As Willow lifted the elixir out of her pocket, Calder burst in. "Honorable Rider, Lord Elsen's army is attacking!" he said.

"Quickly, Uncle. I must hurry," said Willow.

"No," Calder said as he grabbed her arm. "You must come now. We need you."

"But I —" Willow started to say.

Calder's grip was firm. "Now," he said.

Willow let Calder drag her out of the room. They raced downstairs and heard battle cries. Through the windows she saw arrows flying across the sky, some of them tipped with fire. Buildings caught fire, the flames leaping high into the black sky. Men ran here and there, desperately trying to put out the flames.

"I know a secret passageway that's quicker and safe from the arrows," Calder said, leading her away from the men. Obecky, who had been waiting outside for Willow, followed closely behind. It was deserted in this part of Lord Gildenfair's castle, and the sounds of the battle grew muted. "It's through here."

Willow stepped through the door before Calder. Suddenly, it slammed behind her.

"Calder? What are you doing?" Willow said.

"I'm freeing the city from Lord Gildenfair's grasp," Calder replied as he locked the door.

"Let me out!" Willow yelled.

Through a high, barred window Willow heard Obecky whinnying and Calder yelling. Willow jumped up and caught onto the ledge. Her feet hung off the ground while she peered through the bars.

The light of the burning buildings was bright. Willow could see that Calder had tied rope around Obecky's ankles to keep her from escaping.

Unicorns couldn't stand to be tied in any way. Not only did it weaken their powers, it hurt them. Within moments, Obecky couldn't lift her head. When she gave a pained nicker, Willow felt like crying.

"Oh, girl," Willow said as she dropped down from the ledge and slumped on the floor.

What am I going to do? Willow thought. *Arlen is burning. My uncle lies dying. The boy I thought was my friend is a traitor, and I'm locked in here!*

Then Willow felt the amulet around her neck.

"Please find a way out. Help me break down the door," she said.

The amulet radiated heat in Willow's hand. Light shot out from the amethyst, lighting up the window.

Willow jumped up, held onto the bars, and shook them. They wouldn't budge. She dropped back down.

• CHAPTER 10 •

WILLOW HEARD LOUD POUNDING NOISES.

Then she realized — they were trying to break down the city gates!

She hauled herself up and peered out the window again. Through her tears, she spotted a dark shape cutting through the sky.

The amulet warmed around her throat. Bright light pierced the dark sky, illuminating the shape that moved toward her.

That's what the amulet was trying to show me, Willow realized. *Belmont!*

Willow gave a sharp whistle, the kind Jala used to call the falcon. Through the flames, the dark figure circled lower.

"Belmont, what are you doing here?" Willow asked.

The falcon flapped his great wings, searching for a landing spot. There wasn't one. The bird circled, the sky behind him lit by giant, leaping, orange flames.

Willow's hand flew to the amulet around her neck. She felt it getting hotter in her hand and heard Jala's words seep into her mind. "You, my friend, are one of the strongest people I know."

Willow untied the leather strap. Holding onto the window ledge with one hand, she slipped the other hand out through the bars.

"Belmont, catch!" Willow said tossing the amulet high into the air. She held her breath as the amulet arced upward, seeming to move in slow motion. Belmont, with his amazing eyesight and lightning-fast reflexes, swooped down to catch the amulet in his talons.

"Find the others!" Willow shouted. "Give them the amulet, and lead them back here."

The bird gave a raspy screech. Dodging flames and fireballs, he disappeared into the night.

Willow dropped down from the window. All her thoughts, all her hopes, were pinned on the falcon.

Moments later, footsteps sounded outside. At first she thought it was the other Riders. Then she realized these footsteps were heavier than those of her friends.

Calder.

Willow threw herself on the dirty straw pallet on the floor and lay still as the door creaked open.

"Honorable Rider?" Calder said.

Willow recognized the voice instantly. Anger grew inside her, but she remained still.

"I know you're not asleep," he said. "That would be impossible with this battle ringing in your ears. I came back to explain. I owe you that much as an old friend. And we once were good friends, weren't we?"

Willow didn't answer.

"I'm truly sorry for what I've done to you and your unicorn," Calder continued, "but I can't risk you defeating Elsen. He made a deal with me. I give him Arlen and in return he gives me gold — and lots of it. I don't want to be a servant forever, you know. You're lucky, Willow. You've escaped Arlen. Now this is my way out. Willow, can you hear me?"

Still Willow didn't answer.

Calder inched closer. Willow sensed him leaning over her.

"Willow?" he said.

Willow rolled over, kicking out her leg and hooking it behind Calder's knees. Calder dropped to the ground, cursing. Willow pinned his hands together and wrapped her bootlaces tightly around his wrists, knotting them expertly.

"Let me go!" Calder seethed.

"I can't let you betray your own people. Or mine," said Willow. "I'll save Arlen yet."

"It's too late," Calder said. "The army is breaching the walls as we speak. Arlen is already lost."

Willow was furious. "What happened to the Calder I once knew?" she asked. "What happened to my friend?" She bit her lip, trying desperately to control her frustration and disappointment.

"I grew sick of having nothing, that's what happened," Calder replied. "It's fine for you, you're somebody. I'm nothing, but that will all change when Lord Elsen takes the city. You'll see. Give up, Willow. It's already too late."

Willow shook her head. "Unicorn Riders never give up," she said. She turned and strode out of the room, locking the door behind her.

Willow found Obecky, who was barely able to move. She tore the ropes from the unicorn's ankles.

"Work your magic. Heal yourself," Willow said.

Thin gray-blue sparks whirled in the air as Obecky tried to use her magic, but she had been tied for too long, and her magic didn't seem to be working properly. Willow remembered the elixir in her pocket. Would it help Obecky?

She poured some of the liquid into her hand.

I must be careful. Too much could harm her.

Obecky drank. Willow's heart pounded in her chest as she waited for her unicorn to respond to the elixir.

Slowly, Obecky began to return to normal.

"Oh, girl, I'm so sorry," Willow said. She hugged her unicorn's neck. Obecky snorted and tossed her head, her dark mane rippling. "It worked. The elixir worked!"

"Willow, there you are," Quinn said as she came galloping over on Ula. "I thought you were lost or hurt. Then we saw Belmont and he gave us this. We've been looking for you everywhere."

Quinn handed Willow her amulet.

Ellabeth and Krystal arrived on Fayza and Estrella. "Are you all right?" they asked.

"Fine," Willow said. Before she could explain anything, an explosion ripped through the city. The ground shuddered. Dirt and debris were flung everywhere.

"Quick, Obecky! Let's go," Willow said. She leaped onto Obecky's back and galloped through the streets to the city gates. The other Riders followed closely behind. Men were scurrying up and down the burning walls, desperately trying to put out fires and hold off the enemy soldiers.

"Are the walls holding?" Willow asked the captain.

"In most places," he replied. "There was a breach in the northwest corner, but we repaired it."

"They'll break through soon," Krystal said.

Dawn crept over the country. The horizon was lit with orange.

"Right," Willow said. "Let's end this."

• CHAPTER 11 •

"LORD ELSEN'S TROOPS MUST be as exhausted as our men are," Willow said. "Now is the time to strike." She smiled at the other Riders. "And we have just the things to defeat them with. Do we ride as one?"

"We ride as one!" the reply came.

Willow, Quinn, Ellabeth, and Krystal mounted their unicorns.

"Open the gates," Willow commanded the soldiers.

"I'm not letting you go," the captain said. "It's too dangerous."

"Pah!" Ellabeth burst out. "You should know the Unicorn Riders better than that. We're pretty resourceful, you know. Unicorn Riders can do anything."

"For once, I have to agree with you," Krystal said, grinning widely.

"No, that's not the first time you've agreed with me," Ellabeth corrected her. "It's at least the second or third."

"Captain," Willow said, "we'll be fine."

"Please reconsider," the captain begged her. "Lord Elsen's army will eat you for breakfast."

"Come on, Captain," Willow said. "This battle has gone on for long enough. Your people have suffered enough. We can handle this."

The captain looked at Willow thoughtfully, before letting his shoulders sag. "All right," he said. "But be careful. I don't want it on my head if any of you get hurt."

Willow flashed the captain a grateful smile. "We'll be fine," she said.

The Riders cantered out of the gates, then spread out. Estrella sent showers of white magic from her pearly horn, instantly enchanting all the soldiers

who set eyes on her. They dropped their weapons and bowed down to her in adoration.

"Well done," cried Willow.

While Ula galloped toward another group of soldiers, Quinn balanced carefully on her unicorn's back, performing the moves she perfected during her trick-riding lessons. Willow was worried for her, as it was a dangerous move. *Would she be able to stay on Ula's back without falling?* When Quinn knocked the weapons from the soldiers' hands, disarming them, she glanced over at Willow.

Willow breathed a sigh of relief, waving at Quinn in support. The other girl waved back before setting out to disarm another group of soldiers. Krystal had Estrella working her magic nearby.

Willow saw that Ellabeth and Fayza were a blur of color and movement. They galloped toward the soldiers that had been dazed by Estrella and Krystal and disarmed by Quinn and Ula. Ellabeth whirled a lasso around them, catching several at once. She pulled the lasso tight around the men until they fell to the ground, tied up like turkeys for the dinner table.

With a cheer of elation, Ellabeth pulled out another lasso and rode off to capture more soldiers. All the while Fayza's magic whirled, making her and Ellabeth move so fast the men could barely see them.

Willow felt so proud — when they rode as one, they could do anything!

She realized the time was right for her to move in so Obecky could shower her gray-blue sparks of calming magic over the soldiers.

"Come on, girl," Willow told Obecky. "It's our turn."

Before long, the various groups of soldiers sat there, calm and captured and seemingly unbothered by the fact that they had been defeated.

The men of Arlen ran out to help the Riders. They rounded up the enchanted enemy soldiers, who put up no fight but followed every order they were given

as they were marched inside the city gates and locked in the prison.

The Riders found Lord Elsen hiding in his tent.

"You've lost the battle, Lord Elsen," Willow said, striding into his tent, the other Riders behind her. "Your soldiers are all defeated and captured. Do you surrender?"

Lord Elsen's chin rose in the air. "I demand to see Queen Heart," he said.

Beside Willow, Krystal smiled as she crossed her arms. "Oh, I think that can be arranged," said Willow. "She'll want you in Keydell to stand trial for sure."

"Why did you attack Arlen?" Ellabeth asked. "Why harm innocent men and women?"

Lord Elsen sniffed. "I did it for Lord Valerian," he replied proudly. "He has his sights set on Avamay, you know. And on

96

your unicorns. He has spies everywhere. None of you are safe!"

"That's enough!" Willow shouted. She didn't like the way Lord Elsen was talking. It was scaring the others. "Now is not the time for this. You will have your say in Queen Heart's courtroom." She turned to her friends. "And I'm sure Jala will want to hear what Lord Elsen has to say, too."

She called the captain in. "Keep Lord Elsen here under close guard with the others," Willow said.

"It will be my pleasure," the captain said pointedly as he led Lord Elsen away.

"It's not true is it?" Quinn asked as the Riders followed the captain and Lord Elsen out of the tent. "Valerian doesn't have spies everywhere, does he?"

Willow shrugged. "There is a lot we don't know about Valerian," she said, "but I'm sure Queen Heart will get to the bottom of things."

"Lord Valerian is always causing trouble," Krystal said.

"But nothing we can't handle, right?" Ellabeth said. Her eyes blazed with pride as she stroked her unicorn's mane. "Wasn't Fayza brilliant? She's so fast."

"What about Estrella?" Krystal asked. "Those soldiers couldn't resist her enchanting magic."

Willow laughed. "No one ever can," she said. "Well done, Riders. And unicorns. We make a great team. And we'll be ready for Lord Valerian whenever he decides to strike next."

The Riders gave each other a group hug as they agreed.

"Oh, I almost forgot. Where's Belmont?" Willow asked. "We should send a message to Keydell about what has happened here."

"It's already done," Quinn said. "When he brought your amulet to us, I sent him on with a message to Jala asking her to send Queen Heart's army."

"Have you seen Calder?" Quinn asked. "Is he okay?"

"He's locked in one of the rooms at the castle,"

Willow said as she kicked a pebble on the ground. "He'll have to stand trial, too."

Quinn gasped. "I thought he was your friend," she said.

"He was," Willow said sadly, "but not anymore. He's changed. He was poisoning Lord Gildenfair. That's what made him so sick."

"How do you know?" Ellabeth asked.

"I tasted Lord Gildenfair's 'medicine,' and I recognized one of the ingredients. It's greasly poison," said Willow. "I didn't realize it at first, but when Calder locked me up it suddenly hit me. I remembered where I had smelled that horrible scent before. It was when we were doing the obstacle course and the greasly tried to attack Obecky. You can't mistake the smell." She handed Ellabeth the vial of liquid.

Ellabeth sniffed it and pulled away quickly. "Urgh!" she said. "It definitely smells like a greasly."

"Can you Riders see to the rest of these injured soldiers?" Willow asked. "I need to give Lord Gildenfair the elixir, and this time Calder won't be there to stop me," Willow said.

"We'll be fine," Krystal said. "You go before it's too late."

Moments later, Willow sat beside her uncle's bed. He seemed paler than ever.

"Uncle," she said.

Lord Gildenfair didn't move. She reached out and touched his hand. It felt cool and lifeless in her grasp.

Her breath caught in her throat. She was too late.

"U-Uncle?" Willow said.

Lord Gildenfair's eyelids gave the lightest of flutters.

He was alive!

Willow held her uncle's head up and tipped the elixir into his mouth, making sure he swallowed it. Almost instantly the potion began to work. The color returned to Gildenfair's cheeks; the rasping of his breathing eased. His eyes opened and he gazed up at her.

"Thank you, my child. You have saved me," Lord Gildenfair said.

Willow smiled. "You're welcome, Uncle," she said. "And now I need to ask you something."

"Yes?" he replied.

"I need to ask your forgiveness," Willow said. "My anger blinded me to the truth about my family. I realize now how wrong I was. Can you forgive me?"

"Of course," said Lord Gildenfair. "Anything for you, my Flossy."

● CHAPTER 12 ●

IT WAS RAINING HEAVILY when the Riders arrived back in Keydell. The unicorns trotted into the courtyard, their breath snorting steam into the chilly night air. The Riders were wet, tired, and soaked to the skin.

They had stayed two more days in Arlen to ensure the Queen's soldiers arrived to escort Lord Elsen and his men to Keydell for trial. Once everything was in order, the Riders returned home.

Jala rushed out to greet them, holding a lantern under her raincoat as she jogged through the downpour.

"Is all back to normal in Arlen?" she asked.

"Yes," Willow said. "My uncle is recovering, and

we cleared up the problems between us. Arlen is safe once more."

"I'm glad," Jala said. "You've been through a lot, by the sounds of it. Is anyone hurt?"

The Riders all said they were fine.

"We're sure glad to be home," Krystal said.

"I'm glad to have you home," Jala said, and they knew she meant it. "Settle the unicorns in, and then come up to the dining room. I want to hear all about your adventure."

After the unicorns were fed and watered, the girls went to their rooms and changed into clean, dry, uniforms. As they made their way to the dining room, delicious smells wafted through the hallways, making their mouths water.

When Willow stepped into the dining room, the other Riders were already there, along with Jala. Alda was bustling about as usual, laying plates and serving platters piled with food onto the table. Willow licked her lips when she saw what was waiting for her — pheasant and mushroom pie.

"I cooked your favorite dish tonight, lass," Alda said. "To welcome you home."

Willow warmed her hands against the fire before sitting at her place. She glanced around at her friends, watching them silently as they talked and laughed easily among themselves.

It's good to be home, she thought.

Willow plucked a bread roll from the bowl and then passed it to Quinn, who sat beside her.

"Normally, we ride as one," she said, unable to hide her grin, "but tonight I want to know, do we eat as one?"

The other girls giggled. "We eat as one!" they answered in unison.

Willow laughed, too, as she tore the bread roll open and popped a piece of the deliciously soft, still-warm bread into her mouth.

Willow felt Jala's eyes on her. "What?" Willow asked.

Jala smiled. "I was wondering if you found your inner strength in Arlen," she said.

Willow nodded. "I found the strength to forgive, and I have you to thank for it," she said.

"You did that all by yourself," Jala said. She pointed to the amulet around Willow's neck. "Did the amulet help you?"

Willow caressed the amulet. "It sure did," Willow replied. "Um, would it be okay if I kept it?"

"Of course," Jala said. "It's your symbol. I made it for you."

Willow beamed with pride as she helped herself to some pie. "Thank you," she said. "I don't think I could bear to part with it now."

Glossary

adamant (ADAMANT)—not willing to change an opinion or decision

battalion (buh-TAL-yuhn)—a group of soldiers

breach (BREECH)—to make an opening or gap in a structure

brute (BROOT)—a savage or violent person

concoction (kahn-KAHKT-shuhn)—something made by combining several ingredients

elixir (ELIXIR)—a magical liquid that can cure illness or extend life

fortress (FOR-tris)—a place such as a castle that is protected against attack

invade (in-VADE)—to send armed forces into another country on order to take it over

landmark (LAND-mahrk)—objects that help identify a location

omen (OH-muhn)—a sign of something that will happen in the future

precise (pri-SISSE)—very accurate or exact

prosper (PRAHS-pur)—to succeed or thrive

reluctant (ree-LUHK-tuhnt)—hesitant or unwilling to do something

unique (yoo-NEEK)—one of a kind

vial (VYE-uhl)—a very small glass or plastic container used for medicines, perfumes, etc.

Discussion Questions

1. How did the Unicorn Riders support Willow throughout the book?

2. What things happened throughout the book that made you think Calder might not be telling the whole truth?

3. How did the amulet from Jala help Willow throughout the book?

Writing Prompts

1. Willow ended up going to help her uncle, even though she did not want to see him. Do you think she did the right thing? Why or why not?

2. Why was it important for Willow to set a good example for the other Unicorn Riders?

3. It took a lot of courage for Willow to face her uncle. Write about a time when you had to be courageous.

UNICORN RIDERS

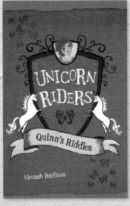

COLLECT THE SERIES!